What's the matter, May?

Written by Juliet Clare Bell
Illustrated by Carl Morris

Collins

Who's in this story?

Listen and say

Anna

Lucy

Download the audio at www.collins.co.uk/839806

Uncle Alex

May

🎧 There was a noise.

"Is that cousin May?" asked Lucy. "Is she here?"

"No," said Anna. "It's only the radio. Can we feed my monkeys?"

"*Again*?" said Lucy.

"Thank you, Lucy. You're my favourite sister," said Anna.

"I'm your *only* sister," said Lucy.

"My only, favourite sister!" said Anna.

"Is that cousin May?" asked Lucy.
"Is she here?"

"No," said Anna. "It's only the wind."

"But I want to see her," said Lucy.

"So do I," said Anna.

"Can we play horse rides?" asked Anna.

"*Again*?" said Lucy.

"Yes," said Anna. "You're my favourite sister ..."

"I know," said Lucy. "OK. Let's go!"

"She's here! She's here!" said Anna. "Hello, May! Hello, Uncle Alex! Lucy is my horse!"

"No, I'm not," said Lucy.

8

"Let's go out on our bikes, May," said Lucy.

"OK," said May.

"But I can't ride a bike," said Anna.

"Don't worry," said Lucy. "You play with Uncle Alex."

9

"That was a great bike ride, May," said Lucy. "Why don't we go and play ..."

"... with my monkeys?" said Anna.

"May and I are too old for monkeys," said Lucy.

"I'm not," said May. "Monkeys are fun. Are they in your bedroom?"

"Oh," said Lucy. "Can I play, too?"

"You're too old," said Anna. "You play with Uncle Alex."

"I don't want to play with Uncle Alex," said Lucy.

May stopped smiling.

"What's the matter, May?" asked Anna.

"I can play with *both* of you!" she said.

"Sorry," said Lucy.

"Sorry," said Anna.

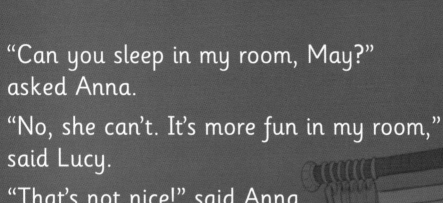

"Can you sleep in my room, May?" asked Anna.

"No, she can't. It's more fun in my room," said Lucy.

"That's not nice!" said Anna.

"What's the matter, May?" asked Lucy.
May said nothing and walked out of
the room.

"That was bad," said Lucy.

"Very bad," said Anna. "Did she go home?"

"I don't know," said Lucy. "Let's try and find her."

They went into the living room.

"I'm sorry, Anna. Your room *is* fun," said Lucy.

"So is yours," said Anna.

"Stop!" said Lucy. "What's *that*?"

"It's May!" said Anna.

"Why don't we make a bed with these?" said May. "And we can all sleep in one room?"

"That's a great idea," said Lucy.

"The BEST idea," said Anna.

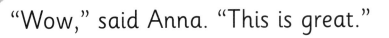

"Wow," said Anna. "This is great."

"It's fantastic," said Lucy. "Do you like it, May?"

May said nothing.

"What's the matter, May?" asked Lucy.

19

May said nothing.
She was *sleeping*!

"... But Anna?" said Lucy. "Can we play a game?"

"A *quiet* game," said Anna.

"Yes. And Anna?" said Lucy. "You're my only, favourite sister, too."

"I know," said Anna. "Let's play!"

Picture dictionary

Listen and repeat

bike ride

cousin

game

monkey

sister

uncle

1 Look and order the story

2 Listen and say

Collins

Published by Collins
An imprint of HarperCollins*Publishers*
Westerhill Road
Bishopbriggs
Glasgow
G64 2QT

HarperCollins*Publishers*
1st Floor, Watermarque Building
Ringsend Road
Dublin 4
Ireland

William Collins' dream of knowledge for all began with the publication of his first book in 1819.

A self-educated mill worker, he not only enriched millions of lives, but also founded a flourishing publishing house. Today, staying true to this spirit, Collins books are packed with inspiration, innovation and practical expertise. They place you at the centre of a world of possibility and give you exactly what you need to explore it.

10 9 8 7 6 5 4 3 2

ISBN 978-0-00-839806-4

Collins® and COBUILD® are registered trademarks of HarperCollins*Publishers* Limited

www.collins.co.uk/elt

British Library Cataloguing in Publication Data

A catalogue record for this publication is available from the British Library.

Author: Juliet Clare Bell
Illustrator: Carl Morris (Beehive)
Series editor: Rebecca Adlard
Publishing manager: Lisa Todd
Product managers: Jennifer Hall and Caroline Green
In-house editor: Alma Puts Keren
Project manager: Emily Hooton
Editor: Frances Amrani
Proofreaders: Natalie Murray and Michael Lamb
Cover designer: Kevin Robbins
Typesetter: 2Hoots Publishing Services Ltd
Audio produced by id audio, London
Reading guide author: Emma Wilkinson
Production controller: Rachel Weaver
Printed and bound by: GPS Group, Slovenia

Download the audio for this book and a reading guide for parents and teachers at www.collins.co.uk/839806